# Smudge

by Rachel Axler

D1562174

A SAMUEL FRENCH ACTING EDITION

SAMUEL
FRENCH
FOUNDED 1830

NEW YORK HOLLYWOOD LONDON TORONTO

SAMUELFRENCH.COM

ISBN 978-0-573-69824-8          Printed in U.S.A.          #29613

### MUSIC USE NOTE

Licensees are solely responsible for obtaining formal written permission from copyright owners to use copyrighted music in the performance of this play and are strongly cautioned to do so. If no such permission is obtained by the licensee, then the licensee must use only original music that the licensee owns and controls. Licensees are solely responsible and liable for all music clearances and shall indemnify the copyright owners of the play and their licensing agent, Samuel French, Inc., against any costs, expenses, losses and liabilities arising from the use of music by licensees.

### IMPORTANT BILLING AND CREDIT REQUIREMENTS

All producers of *SMUDGE must* give credit to the Author of the Play in all programs distributed in connection with performances of the Play, and in all instances in which the title of the Play appears for the purposes of advertising, publicizing or otherwise exploiting the Play and/or a production. The name of the Author *must* appear on a separate line on which no other name appears, immediately following the title and *must* appear in size of type not less than fifty percent of the size of the title type.

In addition the following credit *must* be given in all programs and publicity information distributed in association with this piece:

**Originally produced in New York City in 2010 by**
**Women's Project**
**Julie Crosby, Producing Artistic Director**

**SMUDGE received its world premiere at the Women's Project NYC**

**Developed at The National Playwrights Conference, Eugene O'Neill Theater Center, Waterford, CT.**

**Developed by The Lark Play Development Company, New York City.**

*SMUDGE* was first produced by the Women's Project in New York City on January 3, 2010. The performance was directed by Pam Mackinnon, with sets by Narelle Sissons, costumes by Clint Ramos, lighting by Russell H. Champa, and sound by Asa Wember. Dramaturgy by Megan E. Carter. The production stage manager was Jack Gianino. The cast was as follows:

**COLBY**. . . . . . . . . . . . . . . . . . . . . . . . . . . . . . . . . . . . . . . . . . . Cassie Beck

**NICHOLAS** . . . . . . . . . . . . . . . . . . . . . . . . . . . . . . . . . . . . . . . . Greg Keller

**PETE** . . . . . . . . . . . . . . . . . . . . . . . . . . . . . . . . . . . . . . . . Brian Sgambati

# CHARACTERS

**COLBY** – Late twenties. Female. Married to Nick.

**NICHOLAS** – Late twenties. Male. Married to Colby.

**PETE** – Mid-thirties. Male. Nick's older brother.

## Scene One

(**COLBY** *and* **NICHOLAS** *are in a strange, sterile hospital room.*

*Something about the scale or dimension of the room is a bit askew – maybe it's all a bit too large, swallowing them up.*

**COLBY** *is pregnant.*

*They stare at a small slide, motionless.)*

*(Long pause.)*

**COLBY.** Maybe it's upside-down.

**NICHOLAS.** Breach?

(**COLBY** *looks at him.)*

I think they float around a lot, so you don't have to worry. I mean, how it's positioned right now probably doesn't matter with regard to –

**COLBY.** I meant the picture.

**NICHOLAS.** ...Right.

(**NICHOLAS** *turns the picture around. They stare with renewed interest.)*

*(Pause.)*

**COLBY.** No.
  Right?

**NICHOLAS.** Right. Yeah.
  No.
  It's all...grainy.

**COLBY.** Like a blob.

**NICHOLAS.** Like it's hiding.

7

**COLBY.** Awww…it's our first time not seeing our baby together.

*(They smile at each other.)*

Well. It's okay.

**NICHOLAS.** Yeah?

**COLBY.** I mean…frustrating.

**NICHOLAS.** Yeah.

**COLBY.** We could do it again. Come back in a couple of weeks.

**NICHOLAS.** You know, I think it *is* okay.

**COLBY.** Yeah?

**NICHOLAS.** We can be surprised.

**COLBY.** Yeah.

**NICHOLAS.** I mean, we can be old-fashioned about this.

**COLBY.** Sure. Paint the room green. Buy her yellow clothes. Neutral.

**NICHOLAS.** You said "her."

**COLBY.** What? No.

**NICHOLAS.** No, you did. "Buy her yellow clothes."

**COLBY.** Oh, shit! I did. What does that mean? Maybe she's telling me something. Signaling.

**NICHOLAS.** Or maybe you'd prefer a girl.

**COLBY.** Or maybe it's because I didn't see a penis.

**NICHOLAS.** You saw a fetus?

**COLBY.** No. But I *also* didn't see a penis.

**NICHOLAS.** Yeah, I'd be much more worried if you only saw a penis. I'd hope the two were attached.

*(Pause.)*

**COLBY.** Maybe it's a piece of cheesecake.

**NICHOLAS.** In your uterus?

**COLBY.** I've eaten a LOT of cheesecake recently.

**NICHOLAS.** Three in a week.

**COLBY.** You *counted?*

**NICHOLAS.** You ate them!

COLBY. Ugh. I don't even *like* cheesecake and I can't stop thinking about cheesecake. It's like, I walk down the aisle in the supermarket and I feel it pulling me toward things I would never touch. And making me buy them. And eat a LOT of them.

Ooh! Which reminds me. A woman in Manchester went into a coma. She was like forty. We need to get bananas.

NICHOLAS. ...Were any of those sentences related?

COLBY. Lack of potassium. They discovered, when they did the autopsy or something. Nothing else was wrong with her. One banana, she would have been okay.

NICHOLAS. Food's notoriously bad in England.

COLBY. Manchester, *Vermont.*

NICHOLAS. We'll get bananas.

COLBY. Write it down?

NICHOLAS. I can remember it.

COLBY. Okay, but –

NICHOLAS. Writing it down, look. "Bananas."

COLBY. Put a check next to it.

NICHOLAS. There's nothing else on the page. It stands out.

COLBY. Nick, just –

NICHOLAS. Okay.

(*He does.*)

Look.

COLBY. (*sexy*) Now make it into a chart.

NICHOLAS. ...What kind of chart?

COLBY. Pie.

NICHOLAS. Of course. Large circle. Tiny slice. Statistical probability of lack-of-potassium induced coma for baby Mary—

COLBY. Mary if she's plain. Cassandra if she's beautiful.

NICHOLAS. Jake if she's a boy.

COLBY. She's a girl. She's definitely a girl.

...Nick? I had another one last night.

**NICHOLAS.** Nightmare?

**COLBY.** She came out inside-out. Two-dimensional. I got papercuts.

**NICHOLAS.** Sweetie, it's nerves.

**COLBY.** Flat little cut-out paper doll. She looked like a gingerbread baby. Oooooh – gingerbread….

**NICHOLAS.** Writing it down.

**COLBY.** Ugh! *See?* It's absolutely a girl, and she wants me to be fat.

*(to her stomach)*

We are getting bananas. *Bananas.* You hear me?

Okay, and one cheesecake. But with fruit on top.

Okay, we'll scrape off the fruit.

Just dairy for Mary.

**NICHOLAS.** Cassand –

**COLBY.** *Cassandra.* Cassandra. Unless she's a Mary. …Or a Jake.

*(Pause. They take one last look at the slide.)*

Maybe it's just really, really, really close up.

**NICHOLAS.** Maybe it's abstract.

**COLBY.** We got the one OB who's a frustrated artist.

**NICHOLAS.** Maybe.

**COLBY.** Maybe it's just…smudged.

## Scene Two

(**COLBY** *in a hospital gown. No longer pregnant. She talks to the audience.*)

COLBY. I think I thought it would be bigger.

They hand it to Nick immediately, like they can't wait to get rid of it. Like they think I'd hurt it. Like, "Take a look at the rest of your life," and I'm like: this is a mistake. Right?

It's sort of purplish-grey. And it's skinny, so skinny, except for its head, which is immeasurably huge. I laugh. It's all a big joke.

"Take this mangled mass," I say. "This tired, poor, mangled mass."

"Give me my tiny form," I say. "Where is it? My perfect tiny form."

The nurses won't look me in the eye. They cast concerned glances toward my chin. They whisper. Watch the corners of my mouth for clues. The doctor comes in, three brisk strides. Tells us they need it back now. He talks to a space near my shoulder.

They wash it, dry it off. It's a quiet thing. It whispers.

I count one head. Shading for a torso. A sort of nub. A sort of spike. A point, like a tail, or like a talon, near the bottom. Sort of like a jellyfish. Sort of like something that's been erased. The doctor rushes it away and puts it under a glass, to serve for dinner.

This is how I see it. Under glass, covered in tubes and tape. The eye has opened. Coils of fur grow on it, in odd places.

And my husband loves it.

NICHOLAS. Cassandra.

Little Cassie.

Cassio.

Our pretty babe.

**COLBY.** The open eye is beautiful. Luminous, almost. Blue-green.

It's a disturbing trick of nature, to put that one beautiful eye into that smudge.

The eye is intelligent. Nicholas shows it a Barney puppet, and it blinks.

**NICHOLAS.** There's a girl.

There's a girl.

Who's the prettiest of all?

**COLBY.** There's a feeding tube and a breathing tube and a shitting tube and several other tubes performing mysterious, important functions. The system of tubing inflates and deflates like membrane.

They should have handed it to me.

That first moment – that instant did it. It bonded with Nick.

It doesn't like me. It doesn't cry, but it doesn't really have to. I know. There's jealousy in its eye as it counts my hands, finds itself lacking. It wants my fingers. It dares me to unleash it – lift the glass and tear off the tubes, so it can fly at me and claim my fingers as its own.

**NICHOLAS.** Cassandra.

Little Cassie.

**COLBY.** Maybe it can't cry.

**NICHOLAS.** Cassling,

**COLBY.** Maybe it needs a crying tube.

**NICHOLAS.** Cassie watches me with one eye closed, one all-seeing. Her Caribbean Sea-colored eye.

I want to touch her, my thumb on her cheek, to smooth her skin, stretched so tightly....

**COLBY.** I've been having nightmares again, which means I move in bed. I kick Nicholas one too many times. He moves to the couch.

...They're letting us take it home soon.

## Scene Three

(**NICHOLAS**' *cubicle. Tastefully decorated. Low walls.*)

(**NICHOLAS** *sits in front of the computer, not using it. He goes through a folder of data, highlighting certain lines.*)

(**PETE**, *Nick's older brother and superior – sort of an overgrown frat boy – sticks his head over the cubicle wall.*)

PETE. Workin' hard or hardly workin'?

NICHOLAS. Working pretty hard, actually. I was originally using the P/F method on last year's data –

PETE. Bro. *Rhetorical.* I don't care. The point is not the answer, the point is the wordplay. Like "jumbo shrimp." How do you answer that? You don't. It's rhetorical.

NICHOLAS. Gotcha.

PETE. Ah damn, now you fucked up your big salutation. Hold on – I'll do it anyway:

Bro! Little brutha! Welcome back to the land of the dying-inside!

NICHOLAS. Thanks. You know it's just a few mornings a week, right?

PETE. Yeah, yeah, we'll see about that. Soooo…?

NICHOLAS. How've you been, Pete.

PETE. That's *Uncle* Pete to you, now! And don't ask questions when you're not interested in the answers, 'cause "how've you been?" That's not rhetorical. And personally, I find myself extremely interesting. Like, this morning? *Pooped. Purple.* Shit you not, no pun intended.

And not like a *hue*, you know, not like a *tint* – this thing was like *violet*. I'm standing at the bowl, staring down at this thing and I'm thinking: My god. This is the end. This is how these things happen. You know, Nick? Barely got a cold in 36 years, and suddenly this. I'm thinking: how am I gonna break it to Tara? I've got three boys, they're gonna grow up with no daddy. I'm sweatin' bullets, my life flashing before me in the toilet water, when suddenly it hits me:

**PETE.** *(cont.)* Rocket pops.

> Those red, white and blue popsicles? Had an open box
> of 'em in the freezer and I tried one, turns out they're
> pretty good, wound up eating maybe five or six....
>
> *I tie-dyed my shit.* Scout's honor. Who knew, right?
>
> Once I figured out I wasn't gonna die, it kinda looked
> decorative. Wanted to take a picture or something.
>
> *(Pause.)*

**NICHOLAS.** Look, I'm only here for a few hours, and I've
got tons of reports to go through –

**PETE.** Hold up, Speedy Gonzalez! Jeez. Workhorse much? I
hear there's been an addition to your family.

**NICHOLAS.** *(smiling)* Yeah.

**PETE.** It feel good? Being a dad?

**NICHOLAS.** Yeah. It really does.

**PETE.** Of course it does! Man, I wanted to visit, be there or
something, but you know –

> Euuugh. Right? I mean I saw that shit happen the first
> time with Tara, and next time? For the twins? What's
> got two thumbs and was on the *upper body* side of the
> curtain?
>
> *(thumbs to chest)*
>
> True story.
>
> Aaanyshit, enough of the emotional crap. Boy or girl?

**NICHOLAS.** Girl.

**PETE.** Girl! Of course, you would.

> No, no, it's great – first granddaughter for Ma. She's
> gonna flip. Name?

**NICHOLAS.** Cassandra.

**PETE.** "Cassandra." Cas-SAN – Wow. What, you didn't like
"Aphrodite?"

**NICHOLAS.** I'm…what?

**PETE.** Kidding. I'm kidding. It's a beautiful name.

> *(He snorts.)*
>
> What is that, Greek?

NICHOLAS. I think so, yes.

PETE. Classic. Nice gay name you saddled your daughter with. You know, the boys were dying to hear about their new cousin. Couldn't wait to play ball with him. Had to explain to them that they'd have to wait a coupla years for that. Now I guess I gotta explain to them about girls. To see those little faces…just fall. Tragic.

No offense.

NICHOLAS. How are they?

PETE. Brilliant, all of 'em. Twins went out for Little League – they're too good. Gotta wait for the bigger leagues, I guess. Coach couldn't handle 'em. Older one's doing soccer. Likes to kick stuff, you know. Chip off the ol' cock. More to the point, though, Ma's havin' a connip-tion. Seriously, when were you planning to invite her to see the baby? Says you haven't even sent pictures. You waiting for an engraved invitation or something?

NICHOLAS. Pete, Colby just got out of the hospital. There were complications.

PETE. Complications, shit, we know all about that. Tara had *twins*, you kidding? Had to cut her up and sew her back, but she managed to put on some lipstick and smile for the camera.

NICHOLAS. Your wife's a very strong woman.

PETE. Strong? No, what she is is attractive. Uses something in her hair, makes it bouncy all the time. Even after ten and a half hours labor, I kid you not.

NICHOLAS. She's beautiful, though. Cassandra.

PETE. Yeah?

NICHOLAS. Yeah, she's just –

The color of her –

Her eye color. This…sparkling blue with flecks of green.

PETE. Hey, that's good.

NICHOLAS. Like the Caribbean. This beautiful, pure color.

**PETE.** Aw, sounds like she's gonna be a Daddy's girl, huh? Well, congratulations, bro. You're makin' me want to see pictures. Might just drop by and check her out.

**NICHOLAS.** Sure, sure. I mean she's just…amazing.

**PETE.** You gotta spoil her, you know. Buy her little dresses and cats and shit.

**NICHOLAS.** I'll try.

**PETE.** Yeah, I sometimes wonder what it'd be like to have a girl. Easier at first, harder later, I think. You know, when she gets the "changes." Ah, you'll do great. You guys'll have tea parties where you pretend to eat those little tacos or whatever…with the sugar…you'll know how to do it. Runs in the family. We're good parents, bro. Naturally. In our blood.

*(Some guy-ish gesture of bonding.)*

*(**PETE** motions toward a large stack on **NICK**'s desk.)*

Put you on Family and Fertility; figured that might be right up your alley about now.

**NICHOLAS.** I saw. Thanks.

**PETE.** No sweat. Hey, look, I'm in the 8:15, so I gotta split soon, but two things. One, you're gonna be really excited about. You want to know?

**NICHOLAS.** What?

**PETE.** Welllll….

Just so happens that we've decided on our presenter for the U.N. Symposium. Three guesses.

**NICHOLAS.** You're not doing it?

**PETE.** …What's that, a negative guess? Are you guessing it's me? Strike one.

**NICHOLAS.** I would have thought you were up for it.

**PETE.** I was. But I'm not doing it. Two more guesses.

**NICHOLAS.** Peter. You didn't suggest…me?

**PETE.** What *is* that? Is that a guess? You're a terrible guesser. Yes. It's you. Congratulations. God, you ruin everything.

**NICHOLAS.** But, I –

Really?

*(He's secretly thrilled.)*

But Lee was up for it before me. He has seniority. *You* have seniority. Did Lee say no? Really? I'm going to do the symposium?

**PETE.** Let's get real, Nick. I've got the people skills, but I don't come off all egghead like you. Not really the "analytical speaker" type. And truth be told – Lee? Kind of a dick. So, as a gift to my younger brother –

**NICHOLAS.** Isn't that nepotism?

**PETE.** Noooo, it's not nepotism, because you're not my nephew.

**NICHOLAS.** I'm going to be our presenter at the U.N. Symposium....

**PETE.** Yeah, alright, look, it's not like you're the keynote speaker, okay? You're just gonna stand behind a podium in some cramped little side room and point at shit.

**NICHOLAS.** Wow.

Wow.... Thank you. I, uh...

*(beat)*

...I don't think I can.

**PETE.** What? Of course you can.

**NICHOLAS.** No, I mean, I want to, I definitely want to, but it's so much extra work. I'd have to be out of the house more than I expected, and leaving Colby alone with Cassandra....

**PETE.** Nick. Trust me – that's part of the gift.

Seriously, her eyes might look all Caribbean to you now, but give it a couple days. If you're thinking the baby might be a handful at all, I'm telling you, multiply that by a thousand and that's more the truth. You got a thousand hands? No. So you go to work, avoid it a little, make some money, let the wife do her thing. Did I mention, it comes with a stipend? It comes with a stipend.

*(He looks at his watch.)*

**PETE.** *(cont.)* Shit! Did I tell you I was in the 8:15? What, you wanna get me fired before I can quit?

*(**PETE** begins gathering up papers, then turns.)*

Look, take it, don't take it. No skin off my neck, which by the way I stuck out for you, but no pressure. You really want to turn it down, spend that time with your baby, I can always find another geek. In fact, you know what? Forget it. It's cool.

*(calls over cubicle wall)*

Hey, Lee?

**NICHOLAS.** Wait wait, no no no –

I'll take it.

**PETE.** Yeah?

**NICHOLAS.** Yeah. Yes. I'll do the extra work. It'll be fine.

**PETE.** You sure?

**NICHOLAS.** Yes.

**PETE.** Good, 'cause Lee isn't in today and I'm announcing the presenter in the 8:15. I'll drop in after; we'll talk strategy.

Oh, and two? Call Ma. Like, today. That maternal instinct she discovered once we left the house? Kicking in, big-time. She wants to talk to you about booking flights.

**NICHOLAS.** ...For what?

**PETE.** 'Cause she loves airplanes. What do you think? To see your little Greek baby. Just give her a call, bro. Gotta run. Hasta la pasta.

*(silencing **NICK** before he can reply)*

*Rhetorical.*

## Scene Four

*(**COLBY** sits on the living room floor, a pile of baby clothes around her.*
*She holds up a onesie, studying it from several angles.*
*Long beat.*
*Then she picks up a pair of scissors.*
*Snips off an arm.*
*Surveys her work.*
*In quick succession, she snips off the other arm and both legs. Deposits the sleeves and feet in a growing pile.*
*With a threaded needle, she begins to sew the holes shut.)*

*(**NICK** bursts through the front door, jubilant.)*

**NICHOLAS.** Guess who's going to be the census team presenter at the U.N. Symposium?

**COLBY.** You?

*(**NICK** deflates.)*

**NICHOLAS.** You were supposed to say, "Who."

**COLBY.** Sorry.

*(as if she can't hear him)*

Who?

**NICHOLAS.** …No, now it sounds like you don't know who I am, as opposed to not knowing –

**COLBY.** Okay, I know it's you, moving on. Is that good?

**NICHOLAS.** It's, uh – yeah. It's pretty huge.

**COLBY.** *(still sewing)* Huge like how? Prestigious?

**NICHOLAS.** Yeah. Um, there's a stipend…are you sewing?

**COLBY.** What? Oh. Yeah. Just a little…you know. Doctoring.

**NICHOLAS.** *(delighted)* Wow. That's so…motherly of you.

**COLBY.** So what does the presenter do?

**NICHOLAS.** Well, I stand there, at a lectern or a…rostrum…. Maybe it's a podium. It's usually something raised. A stage. The front of a room – actually, sometimes the rooms themselves are just sort of raked downwards –

**COLBY.** And what do you *do*? What's the presentation about?

**NICHOLAS.** Uh, demographic analysis. In general, like an opening speaker. An overview of the data we've collected over the year, except this one's a big year, 'cause every decade, every ten years –

**COLBY.** I know what a decade is.

**NICHOLAS.** Right. Well, we compile data annually, but every decade there's this bigger overview of trends, this like *uber*-view that spans the entire ten-year period.
And that's this year.

*(Pause.)*

**COLBY.** So, it's a longer presentation than usual?

**NICHOLAS.** No, about the same length of time.

**COLBY.** But to more people.

**NICHOLAS.** No, probably about the same number of, um…. But they're more likely to be…listening? Look, the real difference is that I'll be synthesizing ten times the data, so –

**COLBY.** So it's ten times the work.

*(**COLBY** snips an arm off a onesie.)*

*(**NICHOLAS** watches, a little flustered.)*

**NICHOLAS.** …So it's more prestigious.
You don't find that even a *little* hot? Lots of charts…?
Colb, what are you doing?

**COLBY.** So ten times you being at work with your friends and your brother, and me being here. Alone.

**NICHOLAS.** Not alone. With Cassie.

*(**COLBY** snips a leg off the onesie, aggressively.)*

It's more money. There's a stipend. Is that her new onesie? Why are you –

*(He notices the piles of cut-off onesie limbs for the first time.)*

Have you been cutting off all her sleeves?

**COLBY.** Mm-hmm.

**NICHOLAS.** You should, maybe, not do that.

**COLBY.** It doesn't have limbs, it doesn't need sleeves. So how much longer, per week, would you say, will you have to be at the office?

**NICHOLAS.** We're going to have to buy all new clothes.

**COLBY.** How long at the office?

*(COLBY cuts off another leg, throws it into the pile.)*

**NICHOLAS.** I just think maybe you should leave one or two –

**COLBY.** You're not answering!

*(Pause.)*

**NICHOLAS.** Maybe a few hours. Extra. A week. Maybe I can work from home.

…I don't know if I can work from home.

Colby.

*(He takes the onesie from her, gently.)*

I was thinking…you should visit her with me. I know you haven't been feeling well –

**COLBY.** I said I haven't been feeling up to it.

**NICHOLAS.** Right. Well, but in terms of us spending more time together, and – she really is looking great. Color's back, and…And the nurses were asking about you –

**COLBY.** *(suddenly)* Hey, let's go somewhere. Take a vacation. Europe or something. Cancun. Just while it's in the I.C.U.; we have a few more days, right? Let's get warm. Let's go on a boat.

**NICHOLAS.** Have you been sleeping?

**COLBY.** I have nightmares when I sleep. Come back to bed?

**NICHOLAS.** When you have nightmares, you kick.

*(Pause. They each take a breath. Neither speaks.)*

## Scene Five

*(Complete darkness. From the dark,* **NICHOLAS** *is heard.)*

**NICHOLAS.** All set?

Here we go.

One…two…SURPRISE!

*(***NICHOLAS** *turns on the lights.)*

*(They stand, a baby carriage between them. The carriage is hooked up to several IV drips, machines, laboratory-looking contraptions. Tubes run out of it, draped over metal bars like tentacles. It beeps softly.*

*A crepe-paper banner is draped from the ceiling above it:*

*"IT'S A GIRL!"*

**NICHOLAS** *is wearing a conical party hat.*

**COLBY** *looks a little like she's facing an oncoming truck.)*

*(Pause.)*

I feel like we should sing something.

*(They don't.)*

Well!

Well, well.

*(Pause.)*

*(The carriage continues to beep.)*

**COLBY.** *(indicating the "IT'S A GIRL!" banner)* We might want to leave that there. For clarification.

**NICHOLAS.** Welcome home, Cassandra.

*(They stand there, like an image of American Really Gothic.)*

*(The carriage continues to beep, bleeding into…)*

## Scene Six

(**NICHOLAS**' *cubicle. The unearthly beeps are still fading as* **PETE** *comes around, sits on the desk, eating a bag of chips.*)

**PETE.** Beep, beep, comin' through! Heyyy...TGIF, right?

**NICHOLAS.** It's Tuesday.

**PETE.** Mentally, bro, mentally.

(*He offers the open bag.*)

Chip? These things are awesome. Tara's got us on some diet. Something to do with toxins and pomegranates, I dunno. Veggies, whole grains, toxins, pomegranates. She gave me a three-hour lecture, that's what I remember.

**NICHOLAS.** You know those aren't whole grain chips.

**PETE.** Um, no crap, Shitlock, that's why I'm eating them at work.

(**NICHOLAS** *waves the bag away.*)

So! When do I get to meet Nero?

**NICHOLAS.** Nero...?

**PETE.** The Little Greek! Been waitin' all morning to say that.

(*picking up a paper*)

...What's this? "On Being." Lotta words.

**NICHOLAS.** (*taking it back*) That's just, uh...research.

**PETE.** You going religious on me?

**NICHOLAS.** No, it's.... It's actually philosophy. Sort of. I'm just trying to figure something out.

**PETE.** Yeah, all I know is? There are more letters than numbers on that page, which says to me: Probably not doing work, huh?

**NICHOLAS.** Well, no – it's part of – I mean, it actually could be incorporated into –

**PETE.** *(covering his ears)* Blahblahblahreligioncult, okay, as long as the presentation's good and I don't see you on the 6 o'clock news, we're cool.

Anyway, the million dollar question: You call Ma?

**NICHOLAS.** I, uh –

**PETE.** *(loud buzzer) Ehhhhh!* Not fast enough. The answer was "no," and how do I know that?

*(taking out several small notes)*

Because apparently someone who *knows* whether or not you called her – let's call her "Mom Doe" – has decided that she no longer knows any way to reach you except through me, a.k.a. "she's not going to call you anymore, not unless you call her first, and would that really be so hard," a.k.a. "if that wife of yours could convince you to have a baby, she can certainly get you to pick up the phone," a.k.a. "you must be very busy at work, or perhaps have stopped loving her," a.k.a. I've stopped answering the phone until I get Caller I.D., which FYI you're refunding me for, because it is within your power and your power ALONE to end this.

**NICHOLAS.** Look, I'm sorry she keeps calling you. But Colby's not doing too well, and I don't know if it's, like, post-partum or…but we just need some time as a…as a three-person family before we introduce other people into the mix.

**PETE.** So call Ma and tell her that! I'm sure she'll understand.

*(NICK gives him a look. PETE cracks up.)*

I know, I could barely keep a straight face. Look, send her a few pictures. It's the least you can do. You want to stall, send 'em with a letter, hand-write it, tell her your phone's broken or something. And while you're at it, tell her mine is, too.

**NICHOLAS.** We haven't taken any pictures of Cassie yet.

*(beat)*

**PETE.** Well, that's weird.

**NICHOLAS.** No, it's just –

She's still in that phase where she just…hasn't been home long and isn't used to –

And the flash, you know, with her…aren't baby's eyes delicate? And hers is so big and –

…What?

**PETE.** Oh, shit.

Shit.

Bro. I'm – I don't know what to say.

**NICHOLAS.** What?

**PETE.** Whoa, that is *rough.* I mean, of course. I should've known. All the signs were there – no call, no birth announcement, no pictures…I just, I just never imagined that….

*(He sighs, shakes his head.)*

She looks like *you,* doesn't she?

You just had to go and pass down your douche-face. I mean…. Oh. Man. That poor kid. I didn't even know douche-faces were genetic, 'cause I sure lucked out. But, bro, I would not wish your face on anyone. Especially a girl. Euuugh.

**NICHOLAS.** Okay, can I get back to work now?

**PETE.** You mean back to "figuring something out?"

*(snorts)*

Go for it, Socrates.…Socrates! Now, *there's* a good Greek name! Lost a real opportunity there, bro. Coulda named your daughter Socrates.

No, look, I just want you to know: I'm here for you, fella. Okay? So if you ever want to talk, do not hesitate to give me a holler. Out of your ginormous douche face.

**NICHOLAS.** It's 8:15.

**PETE.** *You're* 8:15.

*(A beat, proud of this retort. Then – )*

Crap!

*(rushing out)*

Take a damn picture of the kid, would you?

## Scene Seven

(**NICHOLAS** *dangles a stuffed toy carrot over the carriage.*)

**NICHOLAS.** Okay, Cass! Do we know what time it is?

(*like a studio audience*)

"Eye exercise time!"

That's right! Left. And right. And left. And right – switch it up, now! – Right. And left. And right. And – okay, wrong, Cass, but you'll get it eventually. You will get it.

Guess that's enough eye work for today. Which means it's tiiiiime toooo…catch it! Catch it! Catch it! Catch it! Catch it! C'mon, catch it!

(**COLBY** *enters, carrying a grocery bag. She watches* **NICK.**)

Catch it! Catch…it! Catch? Catch? Catch? Catch the carrot? Catch? Carrot catch? Carrot carrot? Catch catch?

**COLBY.** You're tormenting it.

(**NICK** *turns quickly, caught.*)

**NICHOLAS.** It's a game.

**COLBY.** For which one of you?

**NICHOLAS.** Cassie likes it. It's her favorite game.

**COLBY.** (*with "air quotes"*) Did "she" tell you that?

**NICHOLAS.** (*"air quotes"*) Don't say "she."

**COLBY.** (*"air quotes"*) You told me to say "she."

**NICHOLAS.** (*NO air quotes*) No, I told you to say she.

**COLBY.** (*"air quotes"*) You have a problem with "this?" "This" is a buffer. "This" is my way of appeasing you semantically, until I can convince myself that something with a PENIS is a girl.

**NICHOLAS.** That's her leg.

(**COLBY** *takes a box out of a shopping bag. Opens it.*)

Is that a cheesecake?

**COLBY.** Yes. Is that a carrot?

**NICHOLAS.** Yes.

**COLBY.** That carrot is creepy.

**NICHOLAS.** Well, that…cheesecake is creepy.

**COLBY.** Correction: This cheesecake is fifteen hundred calories of necessity.

**NICHOLAS.** Jesus. Hey, maybe you should ease up on the… eating habits.

**COLBY.** Meaning?

**NICHOLAS.** You're not pregnant anymore. You barely had an excuse then.

(**COLBY** *picks up a fork. Sticks the fork directly into the box and takes a bite.*)

Perverse.

**COLBY.** No, what's perverse is dangling that thing over that…other thing.

Then again, maybe there's some sort of kinship there. Neither one is anatomically correct.

(*beat*)

**NICHOLAS.** It's a CARROT.

**COLBY.** With a face. It's a *smiling* carrot.

**NICHOLAS.** It's friendly.

**COLBY.** It's creepy. A carrot with a face is creepy. Not to mention completely unrealistic.

**NICHOLAS.** It's also made of terry cloth. If you want a realistic replica of *anything*, I wouldn't suggest looking to the stuffed toys of the world.

**COLBY.** And what if "she" wants to be a vegetarian some day? Prime tenet of vegetarianism, Nick: nothing with a face or a mother. Don't know about the mother, but that carrot has a face.

**NICHOLAS.** Honestly? I'd be much more inclined to listen to your parenting tips if I ever saw you doing any parenting.

**COLBY.** That thing doesn't need a parent. It's got tubes.

*(COLBY continues to eat the cheesecake.)*

NICHOLAS. ...What do you do here? When I'm at work?

COLBY. Sit. Weep. Count the hours 'til I can return to our chaste bed.

NICHOLAS. Seriously.

COLBY. Seriously? I don't know.

NICHOLAS. ...That's your answer?

COLBY. I don't know.

NICHOLAS. You don't know what you do with her?

COLBY. What do you want me to tell you?

NICHOLAS. I want you to tell me what you do. Do you play games? Do you do exercises? Are you even home? Who's watching our daughter?

COLBY. I'm always watching the monitor, Nick. If something goes wrong, trust me –

NICHOLAS. Not the monitor. Cassie. Are you watching Cassie?

Give me a minute-to-minute. The mundane. Do you interact with her?

COLBY. Sure.

NICHOLAS. How?

COLBY. I don't know. Dangle stuff over the crib. Tell her stories. Coo. You know, the usual.

NICHOLAS. Uh-huh. Okay, good. Can you show me?

COLBY. ...I'm eating.

NICHOLAS. Just a little demonstration.

COLBY. You want me to get crumbs in the carriage?

NICHOLAS. Colby, PUT DOWN THE FORK.

*(Pause.)*

*(She does.)*

Now pick up the carrot, dangle it over the crib and play with your daughter.

COLBY. I don't generally use that carrot when –

NICHOLAS. Pick up the carrot! Dangle it –

**COLBY.** That carrot sucks. I'm not touching that carrot.

**NICHOLAS.** You don't look at her.

I've never seen you look at her.

Not once since she's come home.

I don't even think you know what she looks like.

**COLBY.** I know what she looks like.

**NICHOLAS.** No, you don't.

You were so worried about my taking on extra work. But I sit at the office and I can't concentrate, because I'm too busy worrying about whether you're taking care of her.

**COLBY.** You know what – I'm not.

I'm not.

I'm listening to this "beep-beep-beep" that's so ingrained in my brain right now – SO ingrained – I honestly think I'd keep hearing it if it stopped. And I'd just keep sitting here, listening to a phantom monitor, while she died. And you know what else?

That would be fine with me.

*(Pause.)*

**NICHOLAS.** Okay, that's it.

I am DEAD SERIOUS, Colby. You're going to pick up that fucking carrot, and you're going to come over here and DANGLE that fucking carrot over the carriage. And you are going to SMILE. And you are going to CARE. And you're going to tell your daughter a happy story about that fucking carrot, and while you tell that happy fucking carrot story YOU ARE GOING TO LOOK AT YOUR DAUGHTER.

*(Beat. Then, composed.)*

I'll be in the bedroom.

*(NICHOLAS exits.)*

*(COLBY closes her eyes for a moment.
She doesn't want to pick up the carrot.
She picks up the carrot.*

*She REALLY doesn't want to walk over to the carriage.*
*She takes several deep breaths. She takes a step toward*
*the carriage.)*

**COLBY.** *(tentative)* Look at the carrot.

*(another step)*

Look at the carrot...you.

*(another step)*

Here it comes.
A carrot.
With a face.

*(**COLBY** stops, several feet shy of the carriage.)*

Um.
Hi.
Nick said I have to do this.
Maybe you heard him.

*(She extends her arm, so the carrot is just over the carriage.)*

*(She doesn't look.)*

Once upon a time, there was a toymaker. Named...Jim.
Jim said to himself...
"There are toy pandas and puppies and cats of all
kinds, and...
And giraffes and pigs and...even alligators...Pretty
much the entire animal kingdom.
What else could I stuff?
I know – how about a CARROT?"
So Jim made a creepy stuffed carrot and he gave it a
face and everybody lived happily ever after, the end.

*(She pauses, as if expecting something to happen.*
*Nothing happens.*
*She gathers her breath and steps close to the carriage.*
*The room seems to dim.*
*The monitor beeps grow louder, quickening.)*

Did you "like" that story? The same way you "like" this
toy, you...weird...little –

(**COLBY** *looks into the crib – there's a HUGE burst of light. The beeps turn into one long scream. The tubes and IV bag glow bright red.*
**COLBY** *gasps.*
*She backs away from the crib. As she does, the lights recede.*
*She steps toward the crib. Pulses of light.*
*She steps back. Nothing.*
*Terrified.*)

**COLBY.** …Nick?

(**NICHOLAS** *pokes his head in.*)

**NICHOLAS.** You done? Score one for the carrot?

(**COLBY** *continues to stare at the crib.*
*The monitor's beeps are low, almost soothing.*
*This is, somehow, even scarier.*)

Colb?

…She like the story?

**COLBY.** I think she…really didn't.

(**NICHOLAS** *laughs.*)

**NICHOLAS.** Yeah? What, did you make her cry?

(*He moves to the crib.*)

**COLBY.** Nick, watch out –

(**NICHOLAS** *leans over the crib.*
*Nothing happens.*
**COLBY** *watches it all, mute horror.*)

**NICHOLAS.** (*into the crib*) You didn't cry, did you? You never cry.
You never smile, you never cry. Just quiet. Watching.
What are you thinking?
Look at that face. I don't know. Sometimes I see an emotion in there, and I just – I recognize it. And I know she's experiencing things. Taking it all in. Synthesizing the data. The output might not be a direct correlate to the input, not yet, but give it time.
Give her time.

**COLBY.** ...Nick.

**NICHOLAS.** Yeah?

> *(He looks back at* **COLBY**, *kindly.)*

Don't look so worried. The thing is, with the story-telling? It really doesn't have to be a good story. She sees past the words, to the intentions.

I almost feel like.... Like, it may just be that she hasn't smiled yet because so far, she hasn't really found anything that funny.

...If I'm ever at work and she smiles, call me. Okay?

> *(***COLBY*** *nods, dumbly.*
> **NICHOLAS** *takes her hand, then exits.*
> **COLBY** *looks back at the crib.*
> *Takes a step toward it.*
> *The room darkens again, just a shade. The tubes glow faintly. Ominous.*
> **COLBY** *and the crib stare each other down.)*

## Scene Eight

(**NICHOLAS** *at work.* **PETE** *sticks his head over the cubicle wall.*)

**PETE.** Hey, uh, bro. You got a minute.

**NICHOLAS.** I'm actually in the middle of –

**PETE.** No, I'm telling you. You've got a minute. Sixty seconds. Go.

(*Pause.*)

**NICHOLAS.** ...Go where?

**PETE.** "Go" as in "talk." "Go" as in "explain."

(**NICHOLAS** *just stares at him.*)

No? You need a hint? Okay.

(*stretching*)

Ohhh, yawn, yawn, I'm so tired, what?! Is there a pig in here?

**NICHOLAS.** Sorry?

**PETE.** I said, is there a pig in here?

**NICHOLAS.** What are you talking about?

**PETE.** I dunno, you tell me. We got a couple of calls about the new round of surveys. Apparently, someone snuck in a little supplemental.

Anything you maybe wanted to mention?

Weirdo violent questionnaire, fifty-two, fifty-one.... Tick-tick, bro. You're wasting my time and yours. And time is money, which is power, which is money, which neither of us is gonna have pretty soon when we both lose our jobs over this, which is why you better start talking in the next two seconds.

One second.

**NICHOLAS.** It wasn't weird.

**PETE.** Can't hear you.

**NICHOLAS.** It wasn't weird. Or violent. Just a short survey.

**PETE.** Man, swear to crap, I wish we were still kids, so I could beat you up.

(He holds up a copy of the survey.)

It *is* weird. It's, like, gnomes in a cuckoo-clock weird. *And* it's violent, *and* it's no-joke, 100%, honest-to-fuck *long.*

**NICHOLAS.** If you've already seen it, why are you asking me about it?

**PETE.** (reading) "Would you kill a pig? If yes, continue below. If no, turn to page 2."

First question! Would you kill a fucking pig?

**NICHOLAS.** Would you?

**PETE.** Why would I want to kill a pig? I don't even know what you're talking about.

**NICHOLAS.** Then turn to page two.

(Beat. **PETE** does.)

**PETE.** "Is it okay for a hog farmer to kill a pig?"

"Have you ever eaten bacon?"

"Are you a vegetarian-slash-Kosher?"

"Have you ever been a member or groupie of a hard-core or thrash metal band?"

**NICHOLAS.** I was being rigorous.

**PETE.** Oh, here's a good one. This might be my favorite.

(reading)

"Please number the items in the following list from one to twelve, in order of your willingness to kill them, where one is 'most acceptable' and twelve is 'least acceptable.'

A pig. A puppy. A roach. A cow. A horsefly. A horse. A dragonfly. A dragon. A baby. A lobster. A celebrity. A stranger."

**NICHOLAS.** I don't really see what's wrong with that. We have an enormous sample set; we're already asking questions; why not use them as a resource? Get some real answers. It's important to me, Pete.

**PETE.** Well, glad to see Little Nicky lookin' out for numero one, but guess what, bro? *It's not important to the Census Bureau.* Not on their time and not on their dime. Hey, d'ja hear that? Maybe I should skip this statistics shit and become Poet Fucking Laureate. 'Cause you know, that would be important to *me*.

**NICHOLAS.** Pete –

**PETE.** No, and two? You're upsetting people. We got complaints from nearly every district about this, people saying they're not gonna return any of the forms, claiming mental aggravation –

**NICHOLAS.** Because I'm making them think? Asking them to step back for one moment, and consider their personal ethos –

**PETE.** No, you schmuck, it's because you're asking them to KILL things. For sixteen fucking pages!

**NICHOLAS.** But it's not about killing. It's quantitative analysis, and it's about *keeping*. What makes something worth the effort. Is it better if it's antique? Expensive? Beautiful? Historic? If it provides sustenance? If you're homeless, would you chop down a 200-year-old tree to build shelter? If you're freezing, would you use it for firewood? Or other things – rare books? Is anything flammable fair game? What if you're not freezing – what if you're just cold? Is it worth it to warm your hands briefly over the Gutenberg Bible? Or how about just a bunch of blank paper? What if you didn't realize that that blank paper was about to contain the next Great American Novel?

**PETE.** Dude.

All we want to know is race, gender, income, dependents, how far do you fucking commute to work? You want to "figure something out" about people's ethos…es? Fine! Go. Take some time off, but don't accost an entire city!

Seriously. Toolshed. What is *wrong* with you? This is a fireable offense I gotta cover up here, plus you're slacking on the job, don't think I'm the only one who's noticed, reading fucking psychology books –

**NICHOLAS.** Philosophy.

**PETE.** And top it all off, Ma's still calling me, trying to reach you, says you dropped off the face of the earth, she's worried you're dead or worse, and I can't help thinking: Is this my fault? Was I that camel who gave my brother a straw to sip from, and then broke his back? 'Cause I gotta say, I'm doubting my choice to give you that presentation now. And I don't like being doubted. Particularly by myself.

**NICHOLAS.** No. Pete. You're not – You're not wrong about me. I can do the presentation.

**PETE.** Yeah, but why would I still LET you?

*(Pause.)*

**NICHOLAS.** Right.

**PETE.** Fuck yeah, I'm right.

*(Pause. Staredown.)*

Remove the supplementals. All of them. Call anyone who received one. Alert them that there's been a prank. A *prank*. We don't know by who; we're gonna find out. Apologize. I'm talking profuse. Use some of your big philosophy words.

Stop reading philosophy at work.

Call Ma.

*(**PETE** looks at his watch.)*

FYI, this little convo took us five minutes, easy. Did I say "sixty seconds?" Yes, I did. What I did *not* say was "sixty seconds *or more.*"

*(**PETE** looks for something to hit, to release pent-up anger. Finds nothing.)*

Waste of my life, I swear.

## Scene Nine

(**COLBY** *sits in a corner, as far as possible from the carriage, which is being scary again – creepy lighting, weird, angry beeps.*)

**COLBY.** I'm not listening to you.

(*Angry beeps.*)

I'm not listening to you.

(*Angry beeps.*)

La la la la la la la.

(*Mimicking beeps.*)

I'm not paying attention to you.

(*Angry beeps.*)

…Okay, I guess I'm talking to you. But that's it.

(*Particularly angry beeps.*)

You're a violent little creature.

(*Angry beeps.*)

Nick's going to find out, you know. You can't hide your nature from a parent for long. They know. He'll figure it out. Oh – I think I hear him coming, right now! You going to be all "normal" for him?

(*The beeps subside to a gentle rhythm again.*)

Figured.

(**NICHOLAS** *enters. He's holding the carrot toy.*)

**NICHOLAS.** You accidentally hid this in the back of your sock drawer.

**COLBY.** Huh. That *was* an accident. I'll hide it better next time.

(**NICHOLAS** *puts his coat on, as* **COLBY** *watches.*)

**NICHOLAS.** Okay, girls – I'm off. Have fun. Don't do anything I wouldn't do.

**COLBY.** Ha.

**NICHOLAS.** Maybe try to do a couple things I would.

(**COLBY** *smiles wanly.*)

(**NICHOLAS** *approaches her, as if to kiss her goodbye. Instead he hands her the carrot. Exits*)

(**COLBY** *drops the smile, sighs.*)

**COLBY.** Bring it.

(*The lights dim. The tubes glow.*)

(**COLBY** *takes it in.*)

The good thing is, you seem to conserve electricity.

(*The tubes flicker a bit.*)

Why don't you put on your show for Nick? You hiding your little burlesque? Or just saving it for me? Should I be flattered?

(*Beeps, flickering.*)

By the way, you're not getting that carrot back.
I made you something better.
No no, please – don't get up. I'll bring it over there, to you.

(**COLBY** *takes out a crude, creepy ragdoll. It's been cobbled together from the arms and legs of Cassie's onesies. It's kind of grotesque.*)

Here it is. You like it?
More appropriate, I thought.

(*She dangles it over the carriage.*)

I call him Mister Limbs.

(*Looks in. A flash.*)

You jealous of Mister Limbs?

(*Looks in again. Another flash.*)

Mister Limbs has everything you don't. Plus?

(**COLBY** *squeezes Mister Limbs.*)

**COLBY.** *(cont.)* Water-absorbent.

Maybe I could use *you* to mop something up.

Or maybe you'd just Smudge all over the floor.

*(Angry flashes.)*

You *are* jealous. Check out the limbs, Smudge. Useful, right? Guess what?

I've got FOUR of these. Less floppy, too. Two arms, two legs. And look what they're connected to.

*(She wiggles her fingers.)*

TEN of 'em. More than enough to go around. Oh, and –

*(She moves her thumb.)*

Uh-huh. It's opposable.

You know why? Because that's human. That's human physiology.

They should have given you an anatomy class before you arrived. You would have learned something. Because the fact is – and brace yourself, Smudge, 'cause this is reality – Nothing looks like you. Nothing in nature. Nothing is created like you. Not purposely. You are anti-Darwinism.

*(Particularly angry beeps, flickering.)*

That's it? That's your response? Been there, Smudge. What else have you got?

*(Beeps, flickering.)*

Anti-Darwinism! Respond! Parry!

*(Beeps, flickering.)*

You need new material.

*(The doorbell rings.*
**COLBY** *jumps.*
*She stares into the crib.)*

…How did you –

*(She realizes it was the door.)*

COLBY. *(cont.)* Oh.
Coming!

*(COLBY goes to the door, to open it.)*
…Nick?

*(COLBY opens the door. It's PETE.)*

PETE. Alright, where is that little Greek?

COLBY. …Peter. Hi. Shouldn't you be, um.
Hi.

PETE. Hey, Colb! I'm on a mission…from Mom.

*(Adjusts a pair of sunglasses, poses. COLBY doesn't react.)*

*(PETE drops the pose and holds up a camera.)*

I'm here to take a picture. Snap a phoh-toh. I'm Ambassador Click. Where's your next-of-kin? Hear she's a beaut!

COLBY. Why aren't you at work?

PETE. Why aren't *you* at work? Eh? Ehh? Exactly. Look, here's the deal. Special ops. Someone, and I won't say who, but let's just call him "Mister Your Husband," for some reason is crazy and refuses to press his index finger on a tiny button and capture your kid on film. Also, my mother raised her call frequency to every three hours. Thus, as usual, the task falls to me. Got a digital camera and about seven minutes. Rugrat for me to snap? Click-click?

*(COLBY stares at him for a moment.
Then she smiles.)*

COLBY. You know what?
Yeah.
Yeah, I think that might be a really good idea.

PETE. *(thumbs up)* Turbo.
…Microwave's ready.

COLBY. …Sorry?

PETE. It's beeping.

**COLBY.** Oh. Wow. I don't even hear that any….
Um, let me just see if she's –

*(Sparks emanate from the carriage.)*

Yup, I think she's ready for her close-up.

**PETE.** Right in there?

**COLBY.** That's right.

**PETE.** She got her game face on?

**COLBY.** Oh – You'll see.

*(**PETE** steps over to the carriage, camera poised.
He looks inside.
**COLBY** watches him.
A long pause.
Slowly, **PETE** lowers the camera slightly. He still stares
into the crib.
Finally, he puts the camera down entirely. He steps back.
He doesn't meet **COLBY**'s eyes.)*

…Well?

**PETE.** She's, uh –

*(This is a different **PETE**. Gentle.)*

She's beautiful.

**COLBY.** …What?

**PETE.** They grow so fast. God bless.

*(He puts away the unused camera. Heads toward the
door.)*

**COLBY.** Take the picture. Pete. Don't leave. Take the picture.

*(Taunting sparks fly up from the carriage, then stop.)*

Look!

**PETE.** They grow so fast. Yeah.

**COLBY.** No – !

**PETE.** Yeah, take care, Colb.

**COLBY.** No – Wait!

**PETE.** *(leaving)* Give my best to Nick.

**COLBY.** You *work* with Nick!

*(But he's gone.)*

Are you *kidding* me?

*(COLBY stands there for a moment, then rushes over to the carriage.)*

What did you do to Nick's jerk brother, you little jerk?

*(A light flashes up through the tubes, angrily.)*

Oh, sure, *now* you're angry. *Now* you're responsive. A second ago you were "beautiful."

I bet you liked that, didn't you? Well, don't get used to it. You are a freak. You are happenstance. A bunch of entrails in casing. A hot dog. That's what you are – a freaking hot dog.

*(Angry red demon eyes glare through the tubes.)*

Yeah, I know, you're terrifying.

But I can be pretty scary, too.

Know what I've got, Smudge?

*(COLBY holds up a tiny pair of scissors.)*

I've got these.

*(Beeps, flickering.)*

And I could do it.

Just one snip.

Tiny triangle in the tubing.

Like the first peck through the shell of an egg.

SNIP.

Freedom.

*(The tubes rage.)*

I want to scare you. I want to see your hair stand on end. I want to see horror in your little half-face. I want you to scream. I want to hear what your voice sounds like. I want to pinch you until I prove there's blood in there. I want to poke you with a stick.

*(The beeps quicken until they're one steady scream.)*

COLBY. *(cont.)* Move.

MOVE, dammit.

Blink.

Blink!

SHOW ME YOU'RE ALIVE.

*(Everything stops, and* COLBY *draws in a sharp breath, staring into the crib.)*

Nicholas....

Nicholas....

*(*COLBY *runs to the phone. Dials.)*

She smiled.

## Scene Ten

*(NICHOLAS multi-tasks. He's on the phone. He has a
stack of index cards. He has a stack of papers. Most
importantly, he holds the carrot over the crib, desperate.)*

NICHOLAS. Smile!

Smile!

Smile for the carrot, Cass!

Smile!

Smile for the carrot!

It's smiling at you!

*(into phone)*

Hello, this is Nicholas Stillman from the Census
Bureau. There's been a – a prank, maybe you heard
about it? A supplemental questionnai – Ma'am? Hello?

*(Hangs up. Crosses out a name. Back to the crib.)*

You ever think about probability, Cass?

…What is the probability that you think about probability?

It's such a vast range – all the possibilities in the world
– in what probably looks like a tiny space. Zero to one.
You could say it's one. But it's not; it's infinite.

*(phone)*

Hello? Hi, Nick Stillman from the Census Bureau. I'm
calling regarding…. Dinner. Yes. Go enjoy it. With your
two-point-five kids.

*(into phone with carrot, carrot voice)*

"Give my regards to the point-five!"

*(Hangs up. Back to crib.)*

Your heart beats. Your brain functions, and I'm talking
to you and I'm not crazy. Which means you're alive.
Living is empirical. It's scientific. Check off a box –
alive or dead? Yes or no. Zero or one. Living can't be
qualified.

**NICHOLAS.** *(cont.)* You're a one.

I think you're a one.

I'm sure you're a one.

*(with carrot, baby voice)*

Smile at the carrot and you're a one!

*(into phone)*

Good evening, I'm Nick – okay.

*(They've hung up. Mimicking himself, Bela Lugosi-esque.)*

"Good evening!"…Nobody cares. Just you and me, Cassio.

Okay, Family and Fertility.

The American Family and its Demographics.

*(reading from an index card)*

Only seventy-four percent of mothers who gave birth in the United States in the last year spoke English.

…While zero percent of their babies did.

That was a joke.

Still no smile.

Not funny enough?

You in there?

Check off a box for me?

## Scene Eleven

(**COLBY** *is cleaning up around the crib, wiping and spraying.*
*She looks around, then quickly opens a drawer and takes out a cheesecake. She takes out a fork, begins to dig in....*
*Loud beeps.*
*The lights flicker.*)

**COLBY.** *(annoyed)* Oh, come on. I'm *allowed* to eat this. There is nothing inherently bad about cheesecake. And I have exceptional metabolism.

(*A pause. Nothing.*
*She dig into the cheesecake again, more tentatively.*
*The lights flicker.*
*Pissed off,* **COLBY** *puts the fork and cheesecake down.*)

I could sell you to a freak show. Maybe I'll do it before Nick gets home, and I'll tell him you just up and walked away on your little spike and bump.

(*The lights flicker.*)

Well, you're boring me. What kind of fantastic powers are those? Oooh, I can make tubes glow. Sorry to be a critic, but the novelty wears off.

And I am eating this cheesecake.

(**COLBY** *digs in again.*
*A pause, like the tubes are thinking.*
*Suddenly, the carriage puts on a little Gothic light show.*
**COLBY** *puts down the fork.*)

Wow. Hey, that's not bad. Where've you been hiding that?

(*Beeps, flickering.*)

Back to that, are we?

Well, I know. Limited vocabulary.

That was pretty cool, though. Maybe we could harness that. That would make you a lot less boring, wouldn't it?

*(Beeps, flickering.)*

COLBY. *(cont.)* Maybe you're angry because you *want* some cheesecake. Is that it? I can't really put it in that tube for you. Probably stop up something important.

*(She chews, considering.)*

Cheesecake's kind of like you. Not really cheese, not really a cake. Just call it something; give it a name.

I don't love you.

I hope that's okay.

I know you're not too fond of me, either.

*(Beeps, flickering.)*

Nick told me I'm "not open to our bond."

The thing is, you're kind of hard to bond with. Like, "what do you like? What are your favorite activities?... What's that you say? Getting your nutrients through a tube?"

Okay. I guess we can do that together.

*(COLBY *puts down the fork.*
*Gets out a straw. Unwraps it. Sticks it in the cheesecake.*
*Tries to suck her food through it.*)*

...Points for trying?

## Scene Twelve

(**COLBY** *holds Mister Limbs over the carriage. She twitches the doll in the air, like a conductor, in ¾ time. A strange little beeping waltz begins to emanate from the carriage. Sometimes it's hesitant, sometimes it's pretty, sometimes it's strange.*
**COLBY** *begins to sway, still conducting.*
*The waltz responds to her.*
**COLBY** *begins to dance.*
*The waltz begins to dance.*
**COLBY** *gallops with Mister Limbs, conducting.*
*Christmas lights.*
*There's a noise outside.* **COLBY** *hushes the carriage, and the noises subside. She hides the doll.*
**NICK** *enters, home from work.*
**COLBY** *greets him with her eyes. Different.*
**NICK** *stops.*)

NICHOLAS. Are you okay? What – What's going on?

COLBY. …What?

NICHOLAS. What were you just doing?

COLBY. Nothing.

   …Teaching her to waltz.

   *(Pause.)*

NICHOLAS. You're flushed.

COLBY. I was teaching her to waltz, Nick.

   (**NICHOLAS** *looks at her. Pause.*)

NICHOLAS. Have you been doing the eye exercises?

COLBY. They're pedestrian.

NICHOLAS. …I'm sorry?

COLBY. She doesn't need them.

NICHOLAS. But she needs to waltz.

COLBY. Yes.

   I mean, no. But I think she can. Just from her responses to me, it feels like she –

   She has a remarkable capacity for learning.

*(Pause.)*

**NICHOLAS.** Can I see?

**COLBY.** Later. I…I want it be ready.

**NICHOLAS.** Well.

Don't let me stop you.

**COLBY.** Wait –

**NICHOLAS.** What.

*(**COLBY** approaches him.
She raises her arms toward him.)*

You going to teach me to waltz, too?

**COLBY.** I thought you could show me some data.

From your presentation?

*(Slowly, she puts her arms around him. Tries to caress him.)*

A little of what you've been up to?

**NICHOLAS.** I'm stuck on the regression. Haven't gotten to the charts.

**COLBY.** But it's about families. Right? Isn't it?

**NICHOLAS.** Colb.

**COLBY.** It's been so long.

**NICHOLAS.** Colby, I can't.

**COLBY.** Please.

**NICHOLAS.** I don't know the information…well enough yet…. Come on.

**COLBY.** Please. Please, Nick. A little. Infor. Mation –

**NICHOLAS.** Colby –

*(She tries to get into it, grabbing at him with increasing intensity.)*

**COLBY.** Please, Nick. Just a. Little. Chart or. Graph, Nick. Please. Yes. There. Little. Please. Please….

*(**COLBY** leans in close. **NICHOLAS** breaks away.)*

**NICHOLAS.** You were breathing…in rhythm. With the –

*(He indicates the monitor.)*

**COLBY.** I was?

    *(He nods.)*

    …Oh.

    *(Pause.)*

    Is that bad?

    *(Pause.)*

**NICHOLAS.** I'm sorry, I –

    I can't.

**COLBY.** You said you wanted us to bond.

**NICHOLAS.** I did.

**COLBY.** But you don't anymore.

**NICHOLAS.** No, I do.

**COLBY.** But not like this.

**NICHOLAS.** You can't – you can't have both of us, immediately, back, like it's – like it's your right.

    It's not! It's not fair. On or off. Zero or one. Make a decision. You are not a decimal.

    *(NICHOLAS exits.*
    **COLBY** *stands there.)*

### Scene Thirteen

(**COLBY** *sits on the floor, eating cheesecake.*
*It's midday, but the lights are dim. The tubes glow and*
*give off sparks with each bite. She continues eating.*
*The doorbell rings.*
**COLBY** *looks through the eyehole, opens the door.*
*It's* **PETE.**)

COLBY. Hello.

PETE. Look, I don't know how much you know about this,
but if there's one thing I'm exceptionally good at –
and FYI, nuh-uh, there are like six – it's people skills.
Noticing when someone is just…*off*, you know, like
there's something eating away there, and it might be
turning into a situation, and you're his wife so I'm just
gonna be straight here:

I think Nick's freaking out.

He sits there in that cubicle, and if you look from far
away, you know, it looks like he's working, but he's not.
He's thinking. Which, I gotta say, kinda incompatible
with his job. And I think I know what he's thinking
about, too. He's thinking about what I have, and what
Mike in Surveys has – which is, incidentally, no joke,
like four hundred kids, all blond. So many pictures
in that cube you barely see wall. Granted, the guy's
Mormon, but I think he's only got one wife, so what
I'm guessing is, that is one *tired* woman, and not too
surprising she's not in those pictures, right?

Anyway, what was I saying?

COLBY. You're worried about Nick.

PETE. Shhh! Come on.

…Yeah, just a little.

COLBY. Come in.

(**PETE** *does.*)

Didn't bring a camera this time.

PETE. Oh, it's, uh – it's in the shop.

COLBY. Uh-huh.

**PETE.** Yeah, had to get a part replaced. They said they'd
order it special, probably have it ready in two, three
weeks....

**COLBY.** Pete, I know you're lying.

**PETE.** Yeah?

Huh. You're good. Most people can't tell.

*(He notices the box on the floor.)*

What's that?

**COLBY.** ...Cheesecake?

**PETE.** Oooooh.

Cheesecake.

Now, *that,* that is *strictly* off the pomegranate-toxin diet.

**COLBY.** You want to –

**PETE.** Uh-huh.

*(COLBY gets two forks.
Gives him one, then laughs a little.)*

**COLBY.** Plates.

Sorry, I've been –

This is embarrassing. I've been eating, uh –

**PETE.** Straight from the box?

**COLBY.** Yeah.

**PETE.** Hardcore. I'm in.

**COLBY.** Really?

**PETE.** Shit, yeah!

*(COLBY carries it in. PETE rubs his hands together,
excited.)*

I am about to eat cheesecake.

From the box.

*(to the air)*

That okay with you, Tara?

*(beat, listening)*

Huh! Didn't hear her say no.

Cheers.

**COLBY.** …Cheers.

*(They clink forks, each eating a bite. They both melt.)*

Ohhhhh….

**PETE.** Ohhhhh….

Colby, you are a *dream*. Mmmm.

It's good.

**COLBY.** I didn't make it.

**PETE.** Uh, yeah. Obvious. But still good.

*(They eat for a little bit.*
*Chewing.*
*They smile at each other.)*

**COLBY.** So, you think Nick is upset because of our fantastic little boneless creature?

*(**PETE** swallows wrong.)*

**PETE.** *(recovering)* Sorry. What? Not necessari – What?

**COLBY.** It's okay. That's interesting.

I mean, that's good to know.

*(Pause.)*

*(They chew.)*

He still sleeps on the couch.

I think a small part of him really believes it was my fault. Because maybe, I don't know, I was scared before she arrived. Out came this tiny little bundle of skin and worry.

I don't think he's forgiven me.

**PETE.** Aw, I don't think anyone blames you –

**COLBY.** Are you kidding? That wasn't your very first thought when you saw her?

**PETE.** …Can I be honest?

**COLBY.** I don't know. Can you?

**PETE.** It's happened once or twice.

Colb, truth is? I'm not even sure what I saw. I feel like it kind of – morphed, as I was looking.

**COLBY.** Morphed?

**PETE.** Cleared everything out. Like Colon Cleanse for the brain. Didn't have a thought in my head for initial impact, and then I think it was just "damn" for a while, but in a good way, positively, like "daaaaamn."

**COLBY.** Well, the doctors weren't that understanding. What did I eat? What were my activities? Did I do drugs? Am I *sure* I didn't do drugs? Did I maybe do some drugs and forget, because I was, I dunno, on drugs?

**PETE.** Huh.

**COLBY.** And, I mean, those were the *doctors*. What happened to bedside manner? They asked me how long ago I quit smoking, have I ever worked with or near toxic chemicals, at what point in the pregnancy did I stop *jogging*?

*(Pause. She laughs a little.)*

**PETE.** What?

**COLBY.** They asked me if I had any relatives with "physical abnormalities."

…I said, "No, no relatives, but apparently my OB had his head shoved up his ass."

**PETE.** *(impressed)* You said that?

**COLBY.** Mm-hmm.

**PETE.** Col-*bee.* Harsh.

**COLBY.** I mean, Jesus! How about, why didn't *they* notice? Why did nobody warn *me*?

"Undetected…anomaly…one in a million…" BULL-shit. It's not *my* job to have a baby properly. Someone is supposed to help! Isn't someone supposed to help?

Waiting until this thing was out, then whisking it away and grilling me about the few times I smoked up in my suitemate's dorm room; that was *not* helpful.

**PETE.** You ever get caught?

**COLBY.** No.

**PETE.** We always got caught.

**COLBY.** You can't open the windows. It blows out and everyone can smell it a mile away.

**PETE.** Yeah, but then you wind up setting off the smoke alarms….

**COLBY.** Which is when you microwave popcorn 'til it burns, which sets off the alarm anyway, and the butter smell covers everything.

**PETE.** …Where were you when I was an undergrad?

**COLBY.** Point is, I don't know if they mixed anything into the pot. It was almost a decade ago, and I didn't know *then*. But my god, if everyone who ever smoked anything had babies that looked like THAT?

I mean, nobody would ever procreate.

*(Pause.)*

*(They eat.)*

**PETE.** You know, maybe there's a chance it'll be okay.

**COLBY.** What does that mean?

**PETE.** I don't know. I mean, those doctors sounded like dicks, but they're away. In their dick hospital, or whatever. And you're here, and right there, I mean, lying in there, is your…what you said. Your fantastic creature. Your baby.

**COLBY.** No. I didn't say it was a baby.

A baby is something you hold in your arms. That you can wrap in a blanket and show your family and take pictures of and…. And you're supposed to want to take care of it. I mean, biologically, that's why babies are cute. Because they're helpless little spit-up and crap-machines, but somehow nature tricks you into recognizing something of yourself in them. And that's supposed to be your compensation, at least 'til they grow up and become interesting. You know? In the beginning, you don't get much, but you at least get something you can actually touch. Something that… responds.

*(**PETE** and **COLBY** are suddenly very close. Tense.*
*They look at each other.*
*Neither moves.)*

**PETE.** This is, maybe –

**COLBY.** No, you're right –

**PETE.** We probably shouldn't.

> *(Neither moves.)*

> 'Course, and correct me if I'm wrong, we haven't really done anything. What that just there was, to me, was clear and simple. A little reaching-out. No harm no foul.

**COLBY.** No harm.

**PETE.** No foul.

> No foul.
>
> Zero.
>
> None.

> *(Pause.*
> **COLBY** *puts her hand near his face.*
> *Suddenly, they're kissing. A lot.*
> *They break away.)*

> Okay, now we did something.

**COLBY.** Not "we." I did. That was my fault.

**PETE.** No, come on, I was here. I did some of that.

**COLBY.** That was – I just –

**PETE.** No, no worries. All good. Because I mean, here's the thing, right? No harm, no foul? Little harm, one foul. *Little* foul. Foul-*tip*. Right? It's a strike, one strike, bad strike, but we're not out. You follow? Okay. Okay.

**COLBY.** I'm sorry.

**PETE.** *(getting up)* I should really be getting back to the office. Lots of...office to do.

**COLBY.** Okay.

**PETE.** So, just remember what I said. If you notice any-thing. About your...husband...or my brother, either one...being unhappy....

**COLBY.** Right.

**PETE.** Right.

> Jesus!
>
> I'll just.

> *(He exits.)*

## Scene Fourteen

(**NICHOLAS** *stands over the crib. He holds several index cards in one hand, the stuffed carrot in the other. He directs his presentation into the crib.*)

**NICHOLAS.** Good morning, and welcome to the United Nations Symposium. I'm Nicholas Stillman.

Your father.

Today's presentation will show....

This morning's presentation will illustrate how socio-economic and geographic variables.... Variables. Va-ri-a-bulls.

You think I should start with a joke? Something to ease the tension of the...Census Committ – who am I kidding? They're not gonna care, right Cass?

They're not gonna care.

Um, blah blah Caucasians, blah blah Hispanics, single mother blah, changing structure of the Blah-merican fami-blah....

Blah, blah.

Mommy says you respond to her.

I could use some applause after "I'm Nicholas Stillman." You want to clap for me?

"Welcome to the Symposium. I'm Nicholas Stillman."

...That'll probably get applause. It's at the beginning.

*(with carrot)*

Clap, clap, clap.

Thank you, Carrot!

*(directed at the crib, but narrated, like a story)*

Cassandra rests on one swollen cheek. Her skin sags where it has given up. Her eye continues to watch me, always, saying, "I am yours, and you must love me." I look back into the green-blue sea that refuses to change, and I respond:

**NICHOLAS.** *(cont.)* Well.

That sounds simple.

Now reach for the carrot.

Just reach for it.

Just watch it.

Look at it.

Blink at it.

Please.

Grow, Cassie.

Stretch.

Catch the carrot.

Bend.

Sit up!

WALK.

APPLAUD FOR ME, CASSIE.

Why won't you look at me?

Move!

Grow!

Change!

Change, you little monster.

*(**COLBY** enters.*
*Watches **NICHOLAS**, silently.*
*The lights dim, a tiny bit.)*

You monster.

**COLBY.** Nick.

*(**NICHOLAS** turns.*
*They look at each other.*
***COLBY** holds up Mister Limbs.)*

I use this. And, um –

Watch?

*(**COLBY** moves toward the carriage.*
*She looks in.)*

Hello, little secret.

*(The tubes might glow, very very faintly.)*

COLBY. *(cont.)* How's your practicing going? Have you been
practicing?

...She's being quiet.

We're going to do this for Nick, okay?

But don't worry if you don't get it the first time.
Remember, the more you try it, the better it'll get.

He'll understand.

Alright?

Alright.

...Ready, Nick?

NICHOLAS. *(taken in by her tone, watching her in wonder)*
Ready.

COLBY. Okay.

And one-two-three, one-two-three....

*(Silence.*
*COLBY conducts the air with Mister Limbs.*
*She moves slightly, her eyes closed.*
*A soft swaying dance, over the carriage.*
*No lights, no music. Just COLBY moving. It's strange*
*and beautiful.*
*It lasts.*
*It ends.*
*COLBY lowers her hands.*
*Soft, regular beeps.*
*COLBY is silent for a moment, near tears. Smiling.)*

That was it.

Thank you, Cassie.

*(NICHOLAS is still taken in.)*

NICHOLAS. ...What did she do?

*(Pause. COLBY turns to NICK.)*

COLBY. ...What?

NICHOLAS. Cassie. You thanked her.

Did she respond?

**COLBY.** Respond…?

No, she – she did that.

That was all –

*(**NICHOLAS** still watches **COLBY**.)*

You –

You didn't hear…?

**NICHOLAS.** Hear?

**COLBY.** The music…. The music?

**NICHOLAS.** Is it her waltz?

**COLBY.** Yes!

**NICHOLAS.** Oh, I –

I might have…heard? Maybe I – I wasn't listening right?

*(He really wants to have heard.*
***COLBY** senses something is wrong.)*

**COLBY.** Oh. No. Well. We'll do it again.

She'll just do it again.

*(Pause.)*

*(Suddenly, **COLBY** rushes back over to the carriage.)*

We're doing it again! We're doing it again. One-two – just start –

*(The lights glow halfheartedly.)*

There! Do you see, Nick? How she does the –

Maybe she's just being shy.

Cue music!

**NICHOLAS.** I can't hear it. Why can't I hear it?

*(**COLBY** hums a bar. The music comes in very faintly,*
*like a memory.*
*She stops. The music fades.)*

**COLBY.** You're supposed to keep going!

Take it from there!

I already lost my child when you were born; I am *not* losing *you!*

**NICHOLAS.** I wish I could see it. Is it beautiful?

**COLBY.** Come back.

**NICHOLAS.** Are you in there, Cassie?

**COLBY.** Can you see me?

**NICHOLAS.** I want you to be in there.

**COLBY.** Please come back....

## Scene Fifteen

(**NICHOLAS** *stands at a podium. He clicks on a remote control, which projects a slide behind him:*
*"FAMILY STRUCTURE IN THE UNITED STATES: DEMOGRAPHICS AND VARIABLES"*
*U.N. Symposium Presentation, Presenter: Nicholas Stillman")*

**NICHOLAS.** Good morning, and welcome to the United Nations Symposium. I'm Nicholas Stillman.

(*He pauses for applause. There is none.*)

Cassie never clapped there, either.

(*He shuffles his index cards, nervously. Clears his throat. First slide: a regular graph.*)

This is a chart denoting the rising estimated median age at first marriage, "M.A.F.M" for coupled households over the past decade.

(*Slide: The chart, upside down.*)

This is the chart upside-down. You'll notice how the median age now drops.

(*Slide: A cheesecake.*)

This is a cheesecake.

(*Slide: The Caribbean Sea.*)

This is the color of my daughter's eye.

(*Slide: A long decimal.*)

This is the probability that a baby boy born in a rural county of Arkansas, white parents, married, low income, will grow up to be a professional baseball player.

(*Slide: A very long decimal.*)

This is the probability that a dinner plate will fall through a solid table.

We chart probability on a range from zero to one, using every decimal in between. Probability is greyscale.

NICHOLAS. *(cont.)* Living is binary. Zero or one. Black or white. You've got two choices – alive or dead.

It's in direct opposition to statistics.

*(Slide: A vacuous blur of grey.)*

This is my daughter.

She's the grey area.

Which would you choose? Zero or one?

*(He squints into the lights, suddenly very self-conscious.)*

Good morning, and welcome to the United Nations Symposium. I'm...

I'm gonna go call my mother.

*(NICHOLAS exits.)*

*(PETE enters, in a suit. He stands behind the podium and shuffles through the index cards, re-stacking them into a neat pile.*
*He adjusts his tie.*
*Calls off.)*

PETER. Change that slide, please.

*(The back wall goes white.)*

Let them in.

*(The lights shift again, to something more normal for a presentation.*
*PETE speaks to the group.)*

Sorry for the delay, folks. Thanks for bearing with us. Had a little technical glitch, but everything should be working just fine now. Hope you enjoyed the complimentary beverages at our wet bar, a.k.a. the hallway right outside this room.

So, if everyone will please take a seat, we'll get started with the presentation.

I hope you all enjoy this a lot more than I'm going to.

*(PETE nods toward the back of the hall, and clicks on a remote control, which projects a slide behind him:)*

*("FAMILY STRUCTURE IN THE UNITED STATES: DEMOGRAPHICS AND VARIABLES"*

*U.N. Symposium Presentation, Presenter: Peter Stillman")*

*(PETE sighs, composes himself. He nods, and the lights dim around him.*

*The slide changes to Nick's first chart, clear and untouched.*

*PETE's voice begins to fade with the lights.)*

PETER. *(cont.)* This morning's presentation will illustrate how socio-economic and geographic variables relate to and affect the changing structure of the American family....

## Scene Sixteen

(**COLBY** *and* **NICHOLAS** *at home.*
*Regular lighting. Regular beeping.*)

**COLBY.** Nick.

We could try again.

Couldn't we? Try again?

I want a child.

**NICHOLAS.** We have a child.

**COLBY.** Where?

(**NICHOLAS** *looks toward the crib.*
*He makes a decision.*
*He makes a cradle with his arms.*)

**NICHOLAS.** Right here.

**COLBY.** ...Tell me about her.

(*The next section, until the end of the scene, is a sexual*
*fantasy that moves from foreplay through climax.*)

**NICHOLAS.** You're nursing her. Holding her to your breast.
She smells like graham crackers.

**COLBY.** How many arms does she have?

**NICHOLAS.** Two.

**COLBY.** How many legs?

**NICHOLAS.** Two.

**COLBY.** Does she have a body?

**NICHOLAS.** And two eyes. A face. A perfect, tiny face.

**COLBY.** What's she doing now?

**NICHOLAS.** She's reaching out...grabbing your hand.

**COLBY.** She is....

**NICHOLAS.** Wrapping her stubby little fingers around your
thumb.

**COLBY.** Veins spider-webbing through her skin. The tiniest
nails you've ever seen.

**NICHOLAS.** She's squeezing. Trying to put your fingers in
her mouth.

**COLBY.** She has eyebrows. Eyelashes. Gums, but eventually teeth.

**NICHOLAS.** She's saying her first word. It's "Mama."

**COLBY.** I think it's "truck."

**NICHOLAS.** I think it's "octagon."

**COLBY.** She's taking her first step.

**NICHOLAS.** She's leaving us – waving goodbye from the schoolbus.

**COLBY.** It's just her first day of kindergarten.

**NICHOLAS.** Her first day of high school.

**COLBY.** She's bringing home a boy.

**NICHOLAS.** I don't like him.

**COLBY.** The boy dumps her. She cries next to our bed for three nights.

**NICHOLAS.** It's her high school graduation.

**COLBY.** Her first day of college.

**NICHOLAS.** We wave goodbye from the car.

**COLBY.** She's bringing home a girl.

**NICHOLAS.** It's a phase.

*(gradually quickening breath)*

**COLBY.** She writes for the school paper.

**NICHOLAS.** She rows crew.

**COLBY.** Varsity soccer.

**NICHOLAS.** MVP.

**COLBY.** Pre-med!

**NICHOLAS.** How does she manage it all?

**COLBY.** College graduation.

**NICHOLAS.** She travels to foreign countries.

**COLBY.** She gets a great job.

*(Faster, heavier breathing. Hands all over each other.)*

**NICHOLAS.** Med school.

**COLBY.** Law school.

**NICHOLAS.** She's an artist.

COLBY. She's a renaissance woman.

NICHOLAS. She moves across the country.

COLBY. Her first heartbreak.

NICHOLAS. Her second heartbreak.

COLBY. She moves back.

(*rhythmic, lines almost on top of each other*)

NICHOLAS. She meets a man!

COLBY. She gets engaged!

NICHOLAS. She gets married!

COLBY. (*The line itself is an orgasm.*) She's having a ba –
(by)

(*Everything goes silent, the word hanging unfinished in
the air.
The soft electronic beep continues, sterile.
Beep...beep...beep...beep....
They separate.*)

You know what my primary fear was, whenever I used
to think about a child?

I was scared that there'd be something unappealing
about her. To other kids. Something weird or socially
awkward, that would get her teased. Or that she'd be
shy, wouldn't take advantage of things. That nobody
would ask her to the prom. That it would take her until
college before blossoming into something confident.
Beautiful.

Or that she'd...Jesus, that maybe she'd be walking to
school one day and get hurt. Snatched. Something out
of my control.

NICHOLAS. I was always just...scared he'd be exactly like
me.

COLBY. Oh, no. No, I would've liked that.

NICHOLAS. ...Really?

COLBY. Are you kidding?

I would've loved that.

(*Pause.*)

**NICHOLAS.** You know it's going to be hard.

    You know that, right?

**COLBY.** I know.

    Do you know?

**NICHOLAS.** I think I know.

    …It's going to be really hard.

**COLBY.** I really know.

    *(Pause.*
    *An understanding between them.*
    **COLBY** *reaches into the carriage, to touch her baby for the first time.*
    *Unsure of herself.*
    *Like a new mother.*
    *Lights dim.)*

# ABOUT THE PLAYWRIGHT

Rachel Axler's critically acclaimed play, *SMUDGE*, directed by Pam MacKinnon, premiered at Women's Project in January 2010, and was part of the 2008 O'Neill National Playwrights Conference. Her play *ARCHAEOLOGY* premiered at Kitchen Theatre in April 2009. Other plays include *THE WEIGHT OF PAPER* and *THE DISAPPEARANCE CONUNDRUM*. Her plays have been developed through The Dramatists Guild, Lark Play Development Center, Manhattan Theatre Club, The Playwrights Foundation and the O'Neill National Playwrights Conference, and commissioned by South Coast Repertory and Lincoln Center Theater. Humor pieces of hers have been published in The New York Times, In Character, two editions of New Monologues for Women, By Women (Heinemann), and in bathroom stalls across the country. Rachel received two Emmy Awards as a writer for The Daily Show with Jon Stewart on Comedy Central. She currently writes for the NBC sitcom Parks and Recreation. She received her B.A. in English and Theatre from Williams College, and her M.F.A. in Playwriting from UCSD.

# OTHER TITLES AVAILABLE FROM SAMUEL FRENCH

## THE FACULTY ROOM
### Bridget Carpenter

*Black Comedy / 5m, 1f / Interior*

In *The Faculty Room*, Bridget Carpenter explores the darker side of high school life from the inside of that mythic room, the teacher's lounge. English teacher Adam, Drama teacher Zoe and Ethics teacher Bill, along with mysterious new World History teacher Carver, are all taunted by the disembodied voice of Principal Dennis on the P.A. system. Dedicated yet desperate, inspired yet burnt out, hateful yet loving — the teachers of Madison Feury High are a bundle of contradictions in Carpenter's rich portrait. A funny and caustic look at how truly f*cked up the relationships between teachers and students can get, *The Faculty Room* erupts with gunshots, desperate longing, and a growing wave of spiritual fanaticism. Our education system may never recover.

**Winner of the Kesselring Prize for Playwriting.**

"Lively black comedy…A rollercoaster course…Shalwitz gives the evening a snappy, agitated flair. The design supports the script intelligently."
– *City Paper*

"The three lead actors [Bowen, Anderson & Russotto] bring a lot of humor to their roles. The dialogue is sharp."
– *Washingtonian*

"A delightful madhouse [of] over-the-edge teachers…A riot"
– *Arlington Weekly News*

"Witty dialogue & fine acting [in] this engaging play"
– *The Economist.com/Cities Guide*

"Outrageous circumstances. Howard Shalwitz's good-looking production strikes the right tone. Underplayed pretty much to perfection by Michael Willis…Megan Anderson is an appealing presence."
– *Washington Post*

"Cutthroat portrayals by Bowen & Anderson…Woolly should be commended for their unwavering commitment to new work"
– *Washington Times*

SAMUELFRENCH.COM

# OTHER TITLES AVAILABLE FROM SAMUEL FRENCH

## CROOKED

## Catherine Trieschmann

*3f / Dramatic Comedy*

Fourteen year old Laney arrives in Oxford, Mississippi with a twisted back, a mother in crisis and a burning desire to be writer. When she befriends Maribel Purdy, a fervent believer in the power of Jesus Christ to save her from the humiliations of high school, Laney embarks on a hilarious spiritual and sexual journey that challenges her mother's secular worldview and threatens to tear their fragile relationship apart.

"The work of a big accomplished writer's voice…a gem of a discovery."
–*The New York Times*

"Gorgeous almost beyond belief."
–*The London Times*

"This is a wonderfully neat play, at once simple and complex, grappling with big issues - matters of faith, fantasy and the flesh - while keeping its sneakers firmly planted on the suburban topsoil of adolescent angst and domestic frictions."
– *The Daily Telegraph*